THE RUBBER WOMAN

The world of Cardiff's sex trade hits the headlines when a woman is butchered and left for dead. Pauline distributes condoms to the women of the red light district and is known locally as 'the rubber woman'. Sheand Megan, a forensic psychologist, make it their mission to stop more women becoming victims. They don't know it yet, but one of them is already marked out for death.

THE RUBBER WOMAN

Lindsay Ashford

SHORTLIST

First published in 2007 by
Accent Press
This Large Print edition published
2007 by BBC Audiobooks by
arrangement with
Accent Press Ltd

ISBN 978 1 405 62214 1

Printed and bound in Great Britain by
Antony Rowe Ltd., Chippenham, Wiltshire

CHAPTER ONE

Megan Rhys was getting ready for a night in Cardiff's red light district. She dressed carefully. She mustn't give the wrong signals. Scooping her long dark hair off her shoulders, she caught it up in a silver clasp. After a hot day in the city her eye make-up was smudged. She stared at her face in the mirror, seeing it as the punters might see it. Did the kohl eyeliner make her look too tarty?

There was a tight feeling in her stomach. She always got it a few minutes before walking out of the door. Before she'd come to Cardiff, she'd thought nothing could shock her. She couldn't have been more wrong.

Her mobile phone rang out and she grabbed her handbag from the bed.

'Hello.' The female voice at the

other end was husky. Pauline Barrow had been smoking two hundred cigarettes a week for the past thirty years.

'Hi Pauline—you still okay for tonight?'

'Yeah—is nine o'clock all right?' Her gravelly voice had a strong south Wales accent.

'Fine,' Megan replied. 'Shall I meet you by the factory again?'

There was a pause before Pauline answered. 'Yes, but be careful where you park. Did you hear about the stabbing?'

Megan had seen the report on the evening news. A prostitute had been knifed in the factory car park. She had been thrown out of a car and left bleeding on the tarmac. If another woman hadn't heard her screams she would have bled to death.

Since the crackdown on the vice trade, things had become much worse for women who sold sex. There was an election coming and the government wanted votes. 'Make Our Streets Safe' was the slogan on the posters. But the problem wasn't going to go away. The red light district had simply moved to a darker, more dangerous part of the city.

When Megan next spoke to Pauline, night was falling over Cardiff. The last rays of the setting sun were blocked out by the huge factories on the industrial estate. Long shadows fell across the car park where they had agreed to meet. It was deathly silent now that the factory was closed for the night. Megan glanced around her. Suddenly she caught sight of a figure bending over the boot of a car. It was the shape of the head that told her it was Pauline. Her hair, which was dyed a wild shade of red, was gelled and sprayed into a spiky crown. In daylight she looked quite scary. Now she looked like a busy insect, the spikes sticking out from her forehead like antennae.

'Pauline!' Megan called out while she was still a few yards away. She didn't want to scare her by suddenly appearing out of nowhere.

'Hiya, Meg.' Pauline looked up from the box of condoms she was unpacking. 'I've got a new one tonight—called "Virgin's Prayer", would you believe? It's supposed to taste like rum and orange!' She gave a throaty chuckle and Megan smiled.

Despite her scary look, Pauline's laugh was never far away. She gave out condoms to girls on the streets, and their assorted flavours and designs were always good for a giggle. Megan had learned that this was how she broke the ice. It was a way of getting the girls to open up and talk about their lives.

A thin beam from a security light on the wall shone on Pauline's face. She was only ten years older than Megan, but the deep lines round her mouth and eyes made her look well over fifty. She'd worked Cardiff's red light district from the age of fourteen. Selling sex was the only job she'd ever had until two years ago. The police used to call her 'the oldest tart on the beat', but now she was on the other side of the fence. She was an outreach worker, paid by a local charity to help women get off the game.

She was a lucky find. Megan had been sent to Cardiff by her university to find out what effect the crackdown on the sex trade was having. She was there for six weeks, and as she didn't know the city, she needed a guide. Who better to take her into the dark world of Cardiff's vice scene than an ex-prostitute?

'Shall we get started, then?' Pauline handed her a white plastic bag full of condoms and slammed the boot shut. The heels of her boots clicked on the tarmac as she and Megan walked towards the road. Pauline was the shorter of the two, but her snakeskin boots made up for it. She wore tight black jeans tucked into her boots and a white PVC jacket zipped low to reveal her cleavage.

Megan had been surprised at the way she dressed when they'd first met. She would have thought that after a life of selling sex Pauline would be glad to cover up a bit. 'Not my style, love,' Pauline had cackled. 'And besides, the girls can relate to me better if I look like 'em.'

Megan soon realised she was right. On her own first outing she had worn a black hoodie and tracksuit bottoms, trying to make herself blend into the background. But now she wore the sort of thing she might wear for a night out at a club. Not as revealing as Pauline's outfit, but not dowdy either. She hoped she'd got it right. She wanted the girls on the street to feel they could talk to her the way they did to Pauline.

For Megan, the research was

about more than just facts and figures. She'd worked with the police in Birmingham on cases of rape and murder. Three of the victims had been prostitutes, one of them only sixteen years old when she died. The sight of her pale, lifeless eyes staring up from a mortuary slab was something Megan would never be able to forget.

To her, these women were already victims. A crackdown might make the streets safer for some, but not for the prostitutes. It was as if they'd been written off by society. Pauline's charity was the only group she'd come across that seemed to give a damn what became of them.

'That's where they found Jackie Preston.' Pauline cocked her head at the entrance to the car park.

Megan frowned. 'They didn't say on the news if they'd got anyone for it—was it a punter?'

Pauline nodded. 'I went to see her in hospital this afternoon. All she could remember was that he was white and had a local accent. She said he was wearing shades.'

'At night?'

'I know.' Pauline shrugged. 'You'd think she'd have been a bit suspicious, wouldn't you? Thought twice, I mean, about getting in with him.'

'You would,' Megan said. 'And no-one saw the car?'

'It had gone by the time she was found. She says she can't remember what make it was—just that it was dark blue or black.'

'Is she going to be okay?' Megan asked.

Pauline drew in her breath before replying. 'He's ruined her looks,' she said. 'He stabbed her in the face and neck as well as her stomach.' She jerked her head towards the building across the road, where Megan could just make out the figure of a woman standing in a doorway. 'I don't think she'll ever be doing that again—hell of a way to get off the game, though, eh?' Pauline's chest rattled as she made a sound that was a cross between a chuckle and a growl. Her black sense of humour had shocked Megan at first. Now she realised it was Pauline's way of coping with the tragic stories the women told her.

Few of them sold sex out of choice. Some were runaways from children's homes. Others had been forced onto the streets by men who started off as boyfriends but turned out to be violent pimps. Many had a drug habit and sold sex to pay for their next fix.

'What will Jackie Preston do when she gets out of hospital?' Megan asked.

'There's a place for her in the safe house,' Pauline replied. 'She and her kids can live there for a bit till we sort something out. The charity's promised to find her a job in one of their shops.'

Megan nodded slowly. She wondered if Jackie Preston had

thought of giving up the game before she was attacked. Over the past couple of weeks she had put that question to many of the women who worked in the red light district. Most said they would if they could, but gave lots of reasons why they couldn't. Some were afraid of being beaten up by pimps. Even if they went to live somewhere else, they said, the pimps would track them down.

Others said the money was like a drug. They could go shopping in an afternoon, spot something they liked, and know that by the end of the night they could earn enough to buy it. Then there were the women with small children who said that selling sex was the only job that fitted in with looking after their kids.

'Who's that?' Pauline's voice cut across Megan's thoughts. Pauline was staring at a figure on the corner of the street up ahead. It was a woman and she was heading towards a car that had pulled up. But there was something strange about the way she walked. As they got closer, Megan could see that she was on crutches. One of her legs was in plaster from the knee to the ankle.

'She's never . . .' Megan's voice trailed off as they watched the woman climb slowly and painfully into the passenger seat of the car. After a couple of seconds it drove off.

'I know who that was.' Pauline's mouth slid into a twisted smile. 'It's Cheryl Parry. I saw her up the hospital this afternoon when I went to visit Jackie.'

'Why is she . . . I mean how *can* she . . .' Megan's voice faltered as she watched the red tail lights of the car disappear down a side road between two factories.

'Oh, there's plenty of things she can still do with a broken leg, love!' Pauline's cackle cut through the still night air like a rusty saw. 'Blow job, hand relief . . .' She rolled her eyes up at the darkening sky.

'But it's . . . God, it's desperate!' Megan shook her head slowly.

'Oh, I don't suppose she had any choice in the matter,' Pauline said. 'I know her pimp. BJ, they call him. He's a nasty piece of work. I wouldn't be surprised if it was him that did that to her.'

'What?' Megan frowned. 'You're saying he broke her leg and now he's sent her back out on the street?'

'Very likely, yes.' Pauline shrugged. 'He's on crack, see. It makes 'em even more violent, the crack does. He's a bastard, but she's hooked on him. Well, him and the drugs.'

Megan sighed. The pimps had lots of ways of making women their slaves. The worst were the men who lay in wait outside children's homes, luring teenage girls away with promises of new clothes and nightclubs. Starved of love, these girls were easy prey. Within a couple of weeks of running away they'd be on the streets.

Pauline had once been one of this sad band of girls and it made her a bitter enemy of the pimps in the Cardiff patch. They knew she was trying to persuade their women to give up the game and they hated her for it. Last time Megan had gone out with her, they'd had abuse hurled at them by a man cruising past in a flashy car with blacked-out windows. Megan wondered if he was the pimp who'd sent Cheryl Parry out with a broken leg.

'Hiya, Tash!' Pauline called out to a tall woman standing on the pavement across the street. She was wearing thigh-length boots and a low-cut black mini-dress.

As Pauline walked towards her another voice called from the shadows of a doorway: 'Who is it, Tash?' A skinny girl stepped out of the gloom, her arms clasped round her body. She looked nervous, shifting from one foot to the other.

'It's all right,' her friend called over her shoulder, 'it's only the Rubber Woman.'

Megan had heard other women on the streets use this nickname for Pauline. The word 'rubber' was still used around here as slang for a condom, and as Pauline always carried them, the name had stuck. She'd told Megan it made her laugh. 'Makes me sound like one of those blow-up dolls, doesn't it?' she'd cackled when Megan first heard it.

Pauline started chatting to the two prostitutes and Megan was about to cross the street to join them when a car pulled up alongside her. The window slid down silently. She could see a man's eyes, glinting black in the twilight. The rest of his face was in shadow.

'Hello, love,' he said. 'You doing business?'

CHAPTER TWO

Before Megan could open her mouth, Pauline was bounding across the street. 'Piss off, Mullen!' she yelled. 'She's doing research!'

The car door opened and a short, stocky man with a bald patch climbed out. 'Oh, that's what it's called now, is it?' he said, his eyes on Megan. 'You going to introduce us, then, Pauline?'

Pauline's lip curled. 'This is Mick Mullen,' she sneered. '*Sergeant* Mick Mullen—of the Vice Squad.'

Megan's eyebrows arched. She'd had to get clearance from the police to do her research, but she hadn't met this man.

'And you are?' Sergeant Mullen's tone was as rude as Pauline's. He looked Megan up and down like a piece of meat.

'Doctor Megan Rhys,' she said

through gritted teeth. 'Forensic psychologist. I'm doing research on the vice trade in this area and I've had the okay from your boss.' She held his gaze. 'Tell me,' she said, 'is this really the best use of your time?'

He frowned at her. 'What do you mean?'

'Going after the women when it's that nutter with the knife you should be chasing.' She folded her arms across her chest, glaring at him. 'Not right, really, is it, Sergeant?'

His eyes narrowed. 'Let me ask *you* something, Doctor Rhys.' His nostrils flared as he said her name. 'Is it *right* for psychologists to dress like the tarts they're researching?'

Megan took a deep breath before replying. *Don't sink to his level*, she thought. When she spoke, her voice was calm and clear: 'You want to get rid of these women, Sergeant Mullen—*I* want to protect them.'

The policeman swore under his breath, but before he could say more, Pauline stepped between them. 'Shut your face, Mullen!' she hissed. 'You know she's talking sense.' She dug her hand into the plastic bag she was carrying and pulled out a bunch of condoms. 'Here,' she said, thrusting them at him. 'If you haven't got the balls for a manhunt, make yourself useful and hand out a few of these.'

Mullen gave her a tight smile that didn't reach his eyes. 'You're too kind, Pauline!' He tossed the condoms through the window of his car onto the passenger seat and stepped off the pavement. 'Watch yourselves, won't you, girls,' he called over his shoulder. 'Wouldn't do to wind BJ up—know what I mean?' Before either woman could answer he jumped into the car and slammed the door.

Megan looked at Pauline. 'What did he mean by that?'

Pauline shrugged.

'Do you think BJ was the one who

stabbed Jackie Preston?'

'Could be. Maybe he wanted her working for him and she told him to piss off.' The edges of Pauline's mouth turned down. 'It'd be very handy for the cops if they could pin it on him. Mullen's had him in his sights for weeks.' She wrinkled her nose. 'Takes one bastard to know another, I suppose.'

'Obviously no love lost between the two of you.' Megan gave her a sideways glance. 'Is he bent?'

'Not as such,' Pauline grunted. 'Not in the normal way, anyhow. He's evil, is Mullen. He really hates women, that's his problem.' She sniffed as they wound their way down the darkening street. 'He's supposed to go out on patrol with a pal from the copshop, but every now and then he nips out on his own. He gets the girls in the back of the car and scares them shitless. Threatens them with prison or having their kids taken away unless they dish the dirt on their pimps.' She glanced at Megan. 'Doesn't give a toss what the pimps'll do to them if they find out who's dropped them in it.'

Megan frowned. 'Do you have any proof—that he threatens them, I mean?'

'That girl we met earlier—Tash—she showed me bruises once, on her arms. Said he'd pinned her up against a wall.'

Megan's eyes narrowed. 'I'm surprised you haven't shopped him to his bosses.'

Pauline let out a throaty cackle. 'I'm biding my time, love, don't you worry.'

'Does he know you're on to him?'

'Oh yes,' she nodded. 'He also knows I grassed up the bloke who had the job before him. Now he really *was* bent. Used to make the girls give him a blow job instead of getting a fine. That's another reason Mullen hates me so much—for dropping his mate right in it.'

They walked on in silence for a few minutes before spotting another woman lurking in the shadows across the road. Megan went to cross over, but Pauline put a hand on her arm. 'Not her,' she said.

'Why not?' Megan frowned.

'Tell you later,' Pauline whispered, steering her along the pavement to a street corner where two more women were plying their trade. 'This is Tracy and that's Kelly, her sister.'

Megan smiled at the two women who came to greet Pauline. She studied their faces as they took supplies of condoms to stuff into the money belts slung around their hips. Kelly was a pretty girl of about twenty, with long, curly blonde hair and dark eyes. Tracy looked much older. She had the same blonde hair as Kelly but, even in the semi-darkness, Megan could see that her features were ravaged. The lids of her eyes looked swollen and she had dark circles beneath them. Her skin was pitted with acne scars, but there were two long, thin scars on her face as well. One stretched from her left eye to the corner of her mouth and the other ran from her right ear to her nose, following the sharp line of her cheekbone.

As Pauline chatted to the sisters, Megan began to pick up the threads of their lives. Both had small children and shared a house with their mother, who babysat while they were working. Both talked about having a boyfriend and Megan guessed these men were probably also acting as their pimps.

There was so much she wanted to ask them but she had to be careful. The women who worked the streets were always wary of people who asked questions. Most of them had her down as a plain-clothes policewoman. Pauline always put them straight on that, but they took a lot of convincing. If it wasn't for

Pauline, she'd never have got a word out of any of them.

She started with Kelly, who seemed a lot more bouncy and confident than her older sister. First she asked things that didn't sound too nosey, like the length of time it took to get from home to this part of Cardiff. As they talked, she could feel the barriers coming down. The suspicious look in the girl's eyes had gone.

'How did you meet your boyfriend, Kelly?' Megan held her breath. The pimps were what she was most concerned about. The crackdown on the vice trade didn't seem to be hitting them at all. They still controlled the women and used the money they earned to finance drug deals. She wanted to know who they were. How they operated. But most of the women she talked to were very cagey about the men who ran their lives.

'At school,' Kelly replied. 'We've

been together since we were thirteen.'

'Have you ever wanted to . . .' Megan hesitated, unsure how far she could push things. 'You know, leave him? Keep the money you earn for yourself?'

To her surprise, Kelly laughed. 'If I finished with him I'd have to leave home 'cos he'd come looking for me. And anyway,' she shrugged, 'why should I leave? Why should I take my daughter out of a school where she's happy?'

Megan nodded. 'And what about your mum, Kelly? Does she know where you go at nights?'

'Yeah.' The girl brushed a stray lock of blonde hair from her eyes. 'She doesn't like it, but she's okay as long as we never take the punters home. We always do the business in their car, don't we, Trace?'

Her sister nodded, opening her mouth as if she was going to speak. The movement made the scar on the left side of her face twitch. Megan waited a moment, but no words came from Tracy's mouth, just a muffled sound that was a cross between a cough and sigh.

'Mam doesn't like BJ coming round either, does he?' Kelly cast a sidelong glance at her sister, a little frown line showing between her pencil-thin eyebrows. 'She says the rows keep her awake.'

'Rows?' Megan echoed.

Kelly nodded, staring at the pavement.

'Is that a black eye?' It was Pauline who spoke. She reached for Tracy's chin, angling her face so that the weak light of a street lamp shone onto it.

'No—it's just a bit puffy, that's all.' Tracy frowned, pulling away from Pauline. 'I put loads of bloody concealer on before we came out, didn't I, Kell?'

Her sister nodded again. 'He *is* a bastard, though.'

There was a heavy silence. Tracy stared at Kelly as if she'd given away a guilty secret.

'Listen, Tracy, any time you want to talk . . .' Pauline's voice had lost its harsh, rasping edge. She sounded gentle, like a mother with a hurt child. She fished a card from her jacket pocket and put it in Tracy's hand. 'That's my mobile. Ring me, text me, whatever. Doesn't matter what time of night. You hear?'

With a look that said 'time we were off', Pauline took Megan's arm and headed down the street, away from the sisters. When they were out of range she turned to Megan and said, 'Bastard's got a whole bloody stable of 'em, hasn't he?'

'BJ, you mean?' Megan replied.

Pauline was counting on her fingers. 'There's Cheryl Parry—that girl with the broken leg—for one. Tracy Jebb, number two, and I know of at least one other.'

'What about Kelly?' Megan asked.

'They wouldn't have the same . . .'

'No, not her,' Pauline cut in. 'She's all right, Kelly. Got more sense than most. I think her fella's a lazy bastard but he's not a proper pimp. Just takes her money and spends all day in bed smoking dope.'

A car pulled into the kerb just ahead of them. As they watched, a woman got out, smoothed her red mini skirt over her thighs and tottered along the street towards them. She looked older than the other women they'd met that night, and as she got closer Megan realised she'd seen her before. She was the woman Pauline had walked past without speaking to. The one she'd said she'd tell Megan all about later.

The woman was painfully thin. Her halter-neck top revealed bony shoulders and arms like matchsticks. Her eyes darted this way and that like a nervous bird watching out for a cat. Megan suspected she was one of the many crack addicts who worked the streets to get the money for their next fix.

These women were treated like outcasts by the ones who didn't take drugs. It wasn't because they were on crack, but because their habit made them desperate. They'd do anything for the price of a 'rock'. That meant they often charged less than the going rate, which drove the prices down for everyone else.

Megan turned to ask about the woman, but there was a strange look on Pauline's face. There was a deep furrow between her eyebrows and her lips were pulled so hard over her teeth that all the blood had gone out of them.

As the woman passed she gave a sudden jerk of her head and a gob of spit landed at Pauline's feet. Megan stared, open-mouthed, from the girl to Pauline, expecting a torrent of abuse. But Pauline said nothing. She stood, rooted to the spot, just staring into space.

'Who was that?' Megan whispered.

She heard Pauline draw in her breath before answering. 'That was Rosa. She's my daughter.'

CHAPTER THREE

Megan and Pauline were sitting in the all-night café on the edge of the industrial estate. The harsh strip lighting made Pauline's face seem even more lined, and her skin had a yellowish tinge caused by the years of heavy smoking. The only other people in the café were a couple of long-distance lorry drivers whose trucks had made the tables vibrate when they pulled up outside.

Pauline took a new packet of cigarettes from her bag and peeled off the cellophane wrapper. She lit one up and took several drags, staring into her mug of black coffee, as if she was working up to what she had to say.

She and Megan had pounded the streets of the red light district for two hours after bumping into Pauline's daughter. Pauline had clammed up when Megan had asked about Rosa. Then, when it was almost midnight, she'd turned to Megan and said: 'I'm ready for a chat now—shall we go to the greasy spoon?'

The food served in the all-night café was the sort Megan was trying to cut down on. Since she'd been staying in Cardiff she'd put on half a stone. These late-night outings with Pauline nearly always ended with burgers or bacon sandwiches in places like this. Tonight all she'd ordered was a coffee. As she lifted the big white mug to her lips, Pauline began to talk.

'I was fifteen when I had Rosa,' she said, flicking her cigarette into the blue metal ashtray that sat on the table between them. 'I never knew who her father was.' She sniffed.

'Could have been any one of about twenty blokes I had the month I got caught.' She looked up. If she was expecting some sign of shock or disapproval Megan gave her none. She simply returned her gaze, saying nothing, waiting for her to go on.

There were tears in the corners of Pauline's eyes, but the muscles of her face were clenched. She looked as if she was fighting to hold back her feelings. Megan wondered if she'd told this story to anyone else.

'I'd only been on the streets a couple of months. I didn't know it was that easy to get pregnant.' She sent a plume of smoke billowing towards the ceiling. 'Kept working till the day before she was born.' Her head shook slowly. 'Made a fortune, you know. Punters really go for it, the dirty bastards.'

Now it was Megan's turn to shake her head. She hadn't known this— that pregnant prostitutes were a special turn-on for men who paid for sex. *Why?* Her mouth was forming the word when she snapped it shut. She knew in advance what Pauline's answer would be: there would be no words, just a shrug.

There were so many things about this sordid trade that didn't make sense. Like the men who would pay extra for sex without a condom, knowing the girl could be carrying any number of diseases, including AIDS. Did they get some extra kick, she wondered, by dicing with death?

As she watched Pauline light up another cigarette she tried to picture what she must have looked like at fifteen. She thought about the children's homes she'd run away from. Had anyone in those places ever bothered to explain the facts about sex?

Pauline's daughter had been born thirty years ago, but the same old story was being repeated right now, out there on the streets. Girls who were still kids themselves were having more kids. And for what? To grow up with no better hope than their mothers of doing something decent with their lives.

'She was six weeks old when I gave her up.' Pauline was staring at a dirty mark on the wall. 'Never even had a photo of her.'

'How did you find her?' Megan bit her lip.

'Oh, you'll laugh when I tell you.' Pauline's mouth twisted into a half-smile. 'It wasn't long ago. About six months.' Pauline nodded slowly, staring at the wall as if it was a screen showing scenes from her life. 'She was standing on a corner and I went up to her. Tried to give her condoms.'

'What happened?' Megan held her breath.

'She spat in my face.' Pauline shrugged. 'That's what she does every time she sees me. Just spits at me. Can't blame her, I suppose.'

'How did she know . . . I mean,

how did she recognise you?'

'Someone had told her about me. Told her my name. She'd got hold of her birth certificate, see, so she knew who her mother was, but didn't know where I was.'

'But why did she spit at you?' Megan frowned.

'For caring more about strangers than I'd ever cared about her.' Pauline's hand covered her mouth, as if she was afraid her lips would start to tremble with emotion. 'That's what she said. She says it's my fault she's ended up on the game.'

'Why? How could it be your fault if someone else brought her up?'

'She said the folks who adopted her were mean to her. She kept running away. Police kept fetching her back. Then, when she turned sixteen, there was nothing they could do. She got in with a bad crowd and started on dope. That led on to the other stuff. And she had no job, no qualifications . . .' Pauline's mouth turned down at the edges in a look of hopelessness. 'So it was the old story.'

'How often do you see her?'

'Most nights.' Pauline sighed. 'At first she used to ask me for money. I knew it was for drugs. When I said no she cut me dead. She never speaks to me now. I pick up the odd thing about her from the other girls. Sounds like she's speedballing.'

Megan's eyes widened. Speed-balling was the word for mixing heroin and crack. The drugs were injected together in liquid form straight into the user's bloodstream to give a monster high. It was more risky than almost anything out there. Rosa was heading for an early grave.

'And I think she's probably got at least one kid.' Pauline added this in a matter-of-fact voice but her eyes were brimming with tears.

Megan bit her lip. No wonder Pauline was so upset. How awful to think you might have a grandchild. A grandchild you would never get to see.

'If she has got one, it won't be living with her,' Pauline sniffed. 'State she's in no social worker would let her have a kid in the house. Plus she's got bloody BJ on her case.'

Megan looked at her. 'You mean she's another of his women?'

Pauline nodded. 'I only found out last week. Saw her getting into his car. Christ,' she lit up yet another cigarette, shielding the flame with nicotine-stained fingers, 'I was in a state when I was her age, but not nearly the bloody mess that she's in!'

The two women sat in silence for the next few minutes. Pauline dragged on her cigarette, pulling her lips hard around the end of it so that her mouth puckered into deep ridges. Megan didn't know what to say. It must be pure torture, she thought, for her to have to see her daughter out on the streets, night after night, knowing she was on a path to self-destruction. And the child, if there was one—Pauline's own flesh and blood—what would become of him or her if anything happened to Rosa?

Pauline stubbed out the dog-end of her cigarette and scraped her chair noisily as she got to her feet. 'Come on,' she said with a sigh. 'I promised someone a lift home. She's just round the corner, but I might need your help getting her to the car.'

Megan wondered why this woman was being singled out for special treatment. Pauline's duties weren't supposed to include a taxi service for the women who worked the streets. She soon found out why. The woman was so drunk she couldn't stand. She was slumped against a low brick wall, a can of Special Brew in her hand, and a clutch of empty ones lying on the pavement beside her.

'Hiya, Pauline!' she shouted. The words were slurred but Megan could detect a Scottish accent. 'Can ye wait a minute?' The woman tried to get to her feet, swaying dangerously as she did so. 'I need a piss before we go.'

Pauline grabbed her arm before she fell against the sharp edge of the brick wall. 'Okay, love,' she said in low, soothing voice. 'Just do it here. I've got you. No-one'll see. Just mind me sodding boots, that's all.'

Megan whipped her head sideways and stared at the wall. The sound of urine trickling down the pavement was very loud in the quiet street. Suddenly she remembered something Pauline had said to her on her first night in the red light district. She'd been telling her about a woman who'd just been arrested. She said the woman had complained about the back seat of the Vice Squad car being all wet.

'I didn't like to tell her,' Pauline had said with a wink, 'but I know why the seat was like that.' There was a woman, she said, in her mid-forties, who was an alcoholic. She slept rough in an old shed and never bathed or washed. Pauline knew that this woman had been arrested the previous night. 'She must have wet herself on the back seat—and that other girl sat in it!'

Megan had been amazed that anyone like that could operate as a prostitute. Why, she'd asked Pauline, would any man want sex with a woman in that state?

'Oh, you'd be surprised, love,' Pauline had cackled. 'She does all right, old Cora McBride. Takes them up the alley and only charges them a fiver. Some of her blokes just pay her with a can of Special Brew.'

Megan blinked as a stream of urine trickled past along the bottom of the wall. This must be her. This must be Cora McBride.

She had pressed Pauline that first night, wanting to know about the woman's life. What, she asked, had happened to bring her to such an awful state?

Pauline had told her that, like herself, Cora had had a daughter. A little girl called Kirsty. When she was five years old Cora's pimp had beaten the child to death.

Megan heard the trickle stop. Heard Cora grunt like an animal as she hoisted herself up. Christ, she thought. Why? Why are things like that *allowed* to happen? Women controlled by violent men who went on to beat and possibly kill their children . . .

'This has got to stop.' She said the words aloud, to herself, as Pauline hooked her arm under Cora's to help her down the street. But her words were drowned by the sound of a car screeching to a halt beside them.

Megan could hear the throb of a heavy bass beat coming from the sound system inside. The car was a black Dodge Crossfire with alloy wheels and spoilers front and back. The music thumped louder as the window slid down.

Megan could see only the vague shape of a face. Before she could step closer the engine roared and the car sped away.

Something fluttered out of the window as it went. It was something small and white. Pauline bent to pick it up off the pavement. Megan could see that it was the size and shape of a business card. As she watched, Pauline read it, rolled her eyes at the sky, then screwed it up and threw it into the gutter.

CHAPTER FOUR

'Who was that?' Megan bent to pick up the screwed-up ball in the gutter.

'BJ.'

As Pauline spat out the pimp's name Megan smoothed the crumpled white card. It had Pauline's name and mobile phone number printed on it and the logo of the charity she worked for.

'He must have taken it off Tracy Jebb.' Pauline sniffed.

Megan nodded, remembering how Pauline had urged the woman to get in touch any time of the day or night. So BJ had roamed the streets looking for Pauline, just to give her a warning. She wondered what he'd done to poor Tracy. Would she have been given another beating just for having one of Pauline's cards in her pocket?

'Can we go home now?'

Cora McBride was still hanging on to Pauline's arm. She looked a truly pathetic sight. Her hair, long and greasy, hung over the shoulders of a jacket that was too big for her. There were beer stains all down the front of it. She wore a skirt whose pattern clashed violently with the jacket and had a large wet patch over her left thigh. Megan shuddered to think what had made that.

'Come on then, Cora.' Pauline set off down the street with a wink over her shoulder at Megan.

The car park wasn't far away and when they reached it Pauline spread a plastic sheet over the passenger seat before bundling Cora in.

Megan hesitated before getting into her own car. There was so much she wanted to ask Pauline. She wanted to know how she felt about BJ storming up like that. If she was bothered, it didn't show on her face. And she wanted to know about Tracy Jebb. Was Pauline going to go and see her? Check that she was all right?

Cora McBride was cursing loudly as Pauline half pushed, half lifted her into the car. She was ranting about some punter who'd pinched her as they were having sex. She accused Pauline of adding to her bruises. Pauline was laughing it off, making faces at Megan over her shoulder.

Clearly this was not the time to ask

questions. They would have to wait till tomorrow.

'Are you sure you're going to be all right?' Megan asked, fishing in her bag for her car keys.

'Oh sure,' Pauline croaked. 'She'll be fine when I get her home. You get off now. I'll see you tomorrow, yeah?'

Megan drove off, glancing at Pauline's car as she reversed out of the space. The last thing she saw was Cora's bare leg in the open passenger doorway. She'd hitched up her skirt and appeared to be having a good scratch in the region of her crotch. Megan shook her head. She wondered what flea pit Cora was being driven back to. How many years of this sad life lay ahead before the booze or AIDS or some violent punter put her out of her misery?

*   *   *

It was almost two o'clock in the

morning when Megan got back to the flats where she was staying in the smart new development in Cardiff Bay. She looked about her, blinking as she waited for the lift. The plate glass and the flower-decked balconies seemed a world away from the seedy industrial estate where the prostitutes plied their trade.

But a few years ago this place had had exactly the same problem. It was called Tiger Bay then and no-one with any choice in the matter wanted to live there. Rusty cranes threw monster shadows over cramped back-to-back houses. The streets were so dangerous at night that policemen would only go there in twos. And on the corners of those streets were the women selling sex.

At least in those days the women could look out for each other, she thought. Sadists like the one who'd stabbed Jackie Preston would have been far less likely to get away without being seen.

The problem was, of course, that the people in the houses didn't like having prostitutes on the street corners. No-one could blame them for that. Tiger Bay had been cleaned up and the problem had moved to another part of the city. And the people there didn't want it either.

This new crackdown was driving women out like rats from a sewer. But they had to go somewhere. The sex trade was never going to go away.

She'd been to other parts of the country, and had compared the way things worked in cities like Birmingham, Liverpool and Manchester. In some places the pimps ruled the roost and the women were always worse off for it. But in others the sex workers seemed to be in charge of their own lives. They weren't proud of what they did, but at least they weren't having their money taken off them by some thug who fed them drugs to keep them under his thumb.

Getting rid of the pimps was the key, Megan knew that. She'd been to red light districts in other countries—places like Holland and Germany. Tolerance zones, they called them there. They were much safer places than the Cardiff patch. And because the police kept a close eye on the men who went there, rather than the women, the pimps had been squeezed out.

The lift came and Megan stepped in. Her legs, her back, her arms—every bit of her—was weary. As soon as she got through the door of the apartment she took off her clothes. No matter how tired she was, she had to have a shower. She always felt grubby after these evenings with Pauline, as if some of the sleaze she had seen had rubbed off on her.

She reached for the shampoo. It had a strong-scented, male fragrance that made her think of Jonathan. This was his flat. He was a dentist who worked for the police. An expert on identifying bodies from their teeth. She'd met him on a murder case she'd worked on in Wales. They'd had a one-night stand that had made her feel awful.

It wasn't that she didn't fancy him. It was the fact she'd broken her own rules and had sex with a man she barely knew: sex without a condom.

She closed her eyes tight as she rinsed out the shampoo. That night they'd both been spooked by the sight of a very gruesome body in the morgue. They'd gone back to his hotel and started drinking whisky in his room. The sex had been a kind of antidote to the horror of the dead body.

But it had made her feel dirty. The next morning she worried that she might have caught something. After all, she didn't know him. Which made her no better than a prostitute. Worse, really, because she'd done it for free.

Somehow they'd stayed friends.

Well, a bit more than friends. He'd said sorry and in time she'd got over her embarrassment. He'd been to stay with her in Birmingham a couple of times and now he'd lent her his flat. He was working on a murder case in Jamaica and wasn't sure when he'd be back.

She climbed out of the shower and grabbed the big blue bath sheet that hung from the towel rail. As she rubbed herself down she thought about the women she'd met that night. What must it be like, night after night, washing off the smell of strange men? Strange men who might want kinky, risky sex. Men who might hurt you or even kill you without a second thought. She shuddered, remembering Jackie Preston, who was lying in hospital a few miles up the road, her face ruined.

Worn out now, she lay down on Jonathan's king-size bed, still wrapped in the towel. As she closed her eyes she thought about Sergeant Mick Mullen. She wondered if he was really so keen to clear the streets of pimps, or whether it was just a front for his sadism.

God, she thought, those poor women. Caught between the devil and the deep blue sea. She made up her mind at that moment. If Mullen wasn't bothered about finding Jackie Preston's attacker, she'd damn well do it herself. And Pauline would help her. She was sure of that.

Megan had been asleep for only two hours when dawn broke over the city. As colour returned to the pretty window boxes outside the flat, the sun's rays reached into a dirty back alley on the industrial estate across town.

The light fell on black bin bags, ripped open by animals, their contents spilled like guts across the dusty grey concrete. There were used condoms in faded shades of pink and yellow and plastic syringes stained with brown liquid. And at the far end of the alley, stacked against the bin bags, there was something that looked like a shop dummy with a white plastic bag for a hat. But its splayed-out legs were lying in a pool of blood.

There were no flowers to mark the dead woman's resting place. Just a bunch of condoms stuffed between her gaping blue lips.

CHAPTER FIVE

It was nearly midday when Megan woke up. The sun was streaming through a crack in the curtains. It cast a beam across her face, and when she opened her eyes the light was blinding.

Blinking and half asleep, she stumbled into the kitchen. She reached for the kettle and turned on the tap, splashing herself as the spout met the stream of water. While she waited for the kettle to boil she went into the bathroom, peering at her face in the mirror. These late nights were starting to take their toll. There were bags under her dark brown eyes, made worse by the smudged eyeliner she had forgotten to wipe off last night.

She made a cup of strong black coffee and sank onto Jonathan's cream leather sofa. The flat was eerily quiet and she flicked on the TV. It was strange, this need she had for another human voice. At home in Birmingham she never felt alone, even though she'd lived by herself since the break-up of her marriage. What was it about Jonathan's flat that made her feel so uncomfortable?

Something on the television caught her attention. She'd only been vaguely aware of the news, not really taking it in. But suddenly it changed from national stories to the local news from Wales. There was a brief shot of people in white overalls as the first headline was read out.

'A woman's body has been found on a Cardiff industrial estate.' Megan stared as the newsreader's face came back onto the screen. 'The grim discovery follows the stabbing of a prostitute in the same area two days ago.'

Megan gasped as the sign at the entrance to the industrial estate came into view. 'Oh my God,' she said aloud, 'who is it?' The faces of the women she had met last night flashed through her mind.

'The body was found early this morning by a van driver who was dropping off goods at a factory nearby,' the newsreader went on. 'The dead woman has not yet been identified. A post-mortem is being carried out this afternoon. A police spokesman said it was too early to say whether the woman's death is linked to the stabbing of twenty-three-year-old mother-of-two Jackie Preston.'

Megan leapt off the sofa and ran into the bedroom, fumbling in her bag for her mobile. She punched out Pauline's number. Pauline would know. She was bound to. She knew that patch better than anyone. Better than the police.

Someone would have seen that body before the police took it away. News travelled fast among the women who worked the streets. Yes, she thought, Pauline would have heard long before the TV people got the story.

The phone rang six times before the voicemail message cut in. Megan cursed under her breath, waiting for the tone. When she spoke her voice was low and urgent. 'Pauline, it's Megan. I've just seen the news. Can you call me?'

*   *   *

At Cardiff city mortuary Inspector Phil Cameron was standing next to the body that had just been brought in from the alley on the industrial estate. With him was Sergeant Mick Mullen.

The men were about the same age, but Mullen's thinning hair made him look several years older. Cameron towered over him. With his floppy brown fringe and blue eyes, he looked like a tall version of Hugh Grant.

'God, look at the state of her!' Mullen took a step back as the pathologist unzipped the body bag. 'Are those . . .'

'Condoms, yes,' the doctor answered. A silver-haired man of sixty, his face was blank and his voice matter-of-fact. He had seen too many cases of murder to be shocked by anything.

The inspector stared at the bloodless skin of the woman's face. Only her mouth and cheeks could be seen. Her eyes were hidden by the white plastic bag that had been pulled over her head. Its edges were rolled up, giving it the look of a Victorian mob cap. Slowly the doctor eased it off her face.

'Christ!' Mullen gasped. 'It's Pauline bloody Barrow!'

Cameron peered at the staring grey eyes in the lifeless face. 'Not the one who works for the charity?'

Mullen nodded, his lip curled in a look of disgust.

'Poor woman.' Cameron shook his head. 'Just as she was starting to make something of her life.'

'Pah!' Mullen almost spat across the body. 'Bloody troublemaker, that's all she was. No wonder she's ended up on the slab—didn't know when to keep her nose out!'

'Looks as if she was stabbed in the stomach,' the doctor said, carrying on as if he hadn't heard the sergeant's remark. He eased the body onto its side. 'Just the one entry wound.'

'Jackie Preston said her attacker used a kitchen knife,' Cameron said. 'Are we looking at the same kind of weapon here?'

'Very likely,' the doctor replied. 'Interesting, isn't it, that she's fully clothed? And her underwear's still in place. Of course, we'll have to take swabs, but it certainly doesn't look like a run-of-the-mill sex attack.' He looked from one policeman to the other with a smile that lit up his cold, green eyes. 'Not that it's my place to tell you boys your job, of course.'

'What about the condoms?' Cameron asked.

'Yes,' the doctor sniffed. 'I've never seen them in a corpse's *mouth* before. We'll have to look at the gullet—find out if they were put in before or after she died.

'What, you mean she could have choked on them or something?' Mullen blinked as he bent closer to the body.

'We can't rule it out at this stage,' the doctor replied. 'She might have been tortured by her killer or killers before she died. Making her swallow condoms could have been part of that.'

Cameron took a white handkerchief from his pocket. He brought it halfway to his mouth, as if he was on the verge of throwing up. 'Any chance of forensic evidence on the condoms, do you think?'

'We'll swab them all, of course. I haven't counted them, but I'd say there's at least a couple of dozen.'

'Hmm.' Cameron took a step back. 'She'd have had plenty on her, wouldn't she?' He looked at Mullen, who nodded.

'She was a walking bloody Durex factory.'

'And you saw her the night she died?'

'Well . . . yeah.' Mullen shifted his weight from one foot to the other. 'Saw her most nights, though, didn't

I?' He shrugged. 'Hard-faced bitch like that—you'd have to be blind to miss her!'

'Listen, Mick.' Cameron's blue eyes narrowed. 'I know you two didn't get on, but she's dead, for God's sake! Can't you show a bit of respect?'

Mullen grunted. 'She was with that shrink when I saw her, anyway.'

'Shrink?' Cameron frowned.

'You know, that psychologist woman from Birmingham. Doctor Megan what's-her-name.'

'Oh yes, I remember.' Cameron nodded. 'She came to see me a couple of weeks ago.' He stroked his chin with long, manicured fingers. 'Wonder if she saw anything?'

'I'll pull her in if you like,' Mullen said. 'Along with the usual suspects.'

'You do that,' Cameron replied, nodding slowly, 'and send out a team to talk to the women on the streets . . . but of course, you'll have been doing that already, won't you?

For the Jackie Preston case?' He shot a sideways look at Mullen.

Mullen looked away, mumbling something that sounded like, 'Yes, Guv.'

'Hmm.' Cameron turned back to the body on the mortuary table. 'You had plenty of enemies, didn't you, Pauline? Not afraid to stand up to the pimps.'

'No, Guv, she wasn't,' Mullen replied, clearing his throat. 'Not afraid of anyone. That was her trouble, as I said. Looks like she pushed someone too far this time— and I don't think it'll take Sherlock bloody Holmes to work it out.'

Cameron's eyebrows lifted half an inch. 'You think it's BJ, don't you?'

Mullen shrugged. 'I'd put money on it, Guv. He's running more women than any other pimp on the patch. Stands to reason she'd get up his nose.'

'But if this was done by the same person that stabbed Jackie

Preston . . .' Cameron tailed off. He was looking at Mullen, waiting for an answer.

'Could have been, couldn't it, Guv? I mean, Jackie isn't one of his girls, but maybe he was after her. Maybe they'd had a row about it.'

'If that was the case, why wouldn't she have told us?' Cameron's hand was on his chin again, the fingers moving up and down his jaw. 'She said she didn't know her attacker.'

'Hmm.' Mullen thought about this for a moment. 'He might have threatened her.'

'I suppose so.' Cameron frowned. 'Seems unlikely, though, doesn't it? I mean, whoever did it left her for dead. If she knew who it was she could put them away for a long, long stretch. There'd be no reason for her to be afraid, then, would there?'

Mullen shrugged again, running his eyes down the length of Pauline's body. 'You know BJ. He's got his finger in that many pies, I can't see prison stopping him. If he couldn't do the job himself he'd get someone else to do his dirty work.'

Cameron frowned at his sergeant, holding his gaze. 'I hope you're right, Mick—I really do. The sooner we can get scum like BJ behind bars, the better. But if I hear you've played this anything other than straight . . .'

Mullen's face flushed and a little muscle on the side of his head began to twitch. 'Yes, Guv,' he said, in a voice that sounded tired.

'Okay, Doc.' Cameron nodded to the pathologist. 'Give us a bell when you get those results.' He made for the door. As he swung it open and walked out of the room, Sergeant Mullen hung back, his eyes fixed on Pauline Barrow's body.

After a moment he glanced up at the doctor and winked. 'He's not living in the real world,' he muttered. Turning on his heel, he made for the door.

CHAPTER SIX

By two o'clock Megan was pacing round the flat, wondering why Pauline hadn't called back. She couldn't wait any longer. Grabbing her car keys and her jacket she made for the door. She would drive to the industrial estate and find out for herself

As her hand was on the door knob the phone rang. Not her mobile, but the phone in Jonathan's flat. She frowned. It couldn't be Pauline—she only had the mobile number. After five rings the answering machine cut in. She heard someone take a breath before leaving a message. It was a woman's voice.

'Hi Jon, it's Janie. I'm in Cardiff this weekend. Do you fancy getting together? Anyway, give me a bell when you get this. 'Bye darling.'

Megan felt the colour rising up her

neck to her face. She recognised the plummy voice. It was Janie Northcliffe, the woman Jonathan had had a fling with when his marriage broke up. The woman he said he'd finished with six months ago.

'Bye darling. The words rang in Megan's head. Her heart was thudding against her ribs. She wouldn't call him darling unless there was still something going on between them, would she? And why would she want to see him if he'd broken up with her?

She flung open the door and slammed it shut behind her. Charging past the lift, she ran down three flights of stairs and jumped into her car. The tyres squealed as she sped out of the car park. *You're being stupid*, the voice inside her head was saying. And, yes, she knew she was jumping to conclusions. Janie was the kind of person who probably called everyone darling.

And just because she wanted to see Jonathan didn't mean he wanted to see her. Clearly he hadn't told her he was in Jamaica. If Janie had known that she wouldn't have asked to see him this weekend.

She took a deep breath and tried to put it out of her mind. It wasn't as if she and Jonathan were serious or anything. They'd spent a couple of weekends together, that was all. So what if he had other girlfriends—did it really matter?

The churning in her stomach made her realise that, yes, it did. She'd been hurt too much in the past to allow it to happen again. If Jonathan *was* playing around she would drop him like a hot brick. Better to be alone than to be messed about like that.

She noticed with a shock that she'd driven past the entrance to the industrial estate. She'd come halfway across Cardiff without watching where she was going. There was a layby up ahead and she pulled in and turned round. A few minutes later she was there.

The car park looked very different from last night. There was black and yellow police tape all round it and a man in uniform standing guard at the entrance. As Megan slowed down she spotted just one car parked inside the fence. It was Pauline's.

Her heart began to hammer in her chest again. What was Pauline's car doing there? Parked in exactly the same spot it had been in last night when they waved goodbye?

Megan pulled in at the side of the road and as she climbed out of the car she caught sight of a face she knew. It was Kelly Jebb, one of the two blonde sisters she and Pauline had spoken to last night.

Kelly was carrying a bunch of supermarket flowers in her hand. She laid them down at the entrance to the car park. Megan half-walked, half-ran towards her. *My God*, she thought, *is it her sister who's been murdered? Is that what BJ did after throwing the calling card at Pauline?*

'Kelly,' she gasped, tugging at the woman's arm. 'Who is it? Who was killed?'

Kelly turned to her. Her eyes were glassy with tears and there was a frown line between her eyebrows. 'You don't know?' Her voice was a whisper.

Megan shook her head, panic rising in her chest. 'I tried Pauline but she hasn't called back—that's her car, isn't it? Do you know where she is?'

'She's dead.' The words hung in the air like gun smoke.

'Dead?' Megan took a step back, shaking her head. 'But she can't be! That's her car—she was in it when I saw her last night. She was on her way home . . .'

'Well, she never got there.' Kelly bit her lip to stop it trembling. 'They found her in that alley.' She jerked

66

her head to the far side of the car park. Megan could just see a gap in the walls with what looked like a black dustbin liner propped against one side of it. As she stared a man in white forensic overalls came out. He was carrying something in a clear plastic bag.

Kelly rolled her eyes at the sight of him. 'Haven't got a bloody clue, that lot. I asked 'em when they were all here, holding people back while they took her body away. "Have you got the bastard, then?" I says.' She blinked tears from her eyes. 'Course they bloody haven't!'

Megan was watching the man in the white suit but not seeing. She was playing back the scene from last night in her mind's eye. That last view of Pauline waving at her from the car. Cora McBride in the passenger seat. *Cora McBride*.

'She was with someone when I left her.' Megan felt a trickle of sweat run down the back of her neck as she told Kelly about the woman Pauline had offered a lift to. 'She was off her face. Couldn't even walk down the street without help. You don't think she could have . . .'

Kelly shook her head. 'Not Cora. She's a total piss-head, but she wouldn't hurt a fly.'

'No, I didn't mean that.' Megan was breathing fast. 'She must have seen something, mustn't she? Where is she now? How did she get home? Do you know where she lives?'

Kelly nodded. 'She dosses down in an old shed behind the scrap yard.' She pointed to the opposite end of the industrial estate, where the tip of a pile of rusting cars could be seen above the roofline of the factories.

'Can you take me? We can go in my car.'

Kelly glanced up and down the street. It was a furtive look, as if she was afraid of being seen. 'Okay— but I haven't got long. I've got to pick my little girl up from school at half past three.'

As they drove Megan was thinking of the car that had pulled up last night outside the greasy spoon café. Should she tell Kelly that her sister's pimp had been one of the last people to see Pauline alive? Would she still be willing to help if she thought her sister might be dragged into a murder enquiry?

She glanced at Kelly out of the corner of her eye. No, she thought, best to keep quiet for now. Wait and see what Cora McBride has to say.

There was a vicious-looking German Shepherd dog guarding the gates of the scrap metal yard. Kelly told Megan to pull in a few yards further up the road. 'We'll have to get round the back this way,' she said, pointing to a narrow path with straggling privet bushes growing each side of it.

As they picked their way through mud, broken bottles and rusting lager cans they could hear the dog barking frantically on the other side of the fence.

'Do you think anyone can see us?' Megan asked, stepping sideways to avoid a big pothole full of oily water. She wondered how on earth Cora McBride managed to get down this path at night without doing herself a serious injury.

Kelly shook her head. 'The bushes are too high. Don't worry about the mutt—he barks at anything that moves. They won't take no notice.'

The first sign of the shed was a wooden door lying on the ground a few yards ahead of them. It looked as if it had been thrown down as something to step on to avoid the worst of the mud. The shed itself was so overgrown with ivy it was hard to tell there was a building there at all.

As they got nearer Megan could see that the only window had been smashed and plastic bags had been stuffed between the broken shards of glass. Fish and chip papers and cans of Special Brew lay in a heap outside the door, which hung at a crazy angle, as if it was about to fall off its hinges. Megan took a step closer and put out her hand to knock.

'No point doing that!' Kelly edged round her, careful not to step into the mud. She lifted the metal latch and pushed it open. The smell made them both put their hands to their mouths.

Inside it was so dark it was difficult to see if there was anyone there. As Megan's eyes got used to it, she could make out a bundle of something on the floor, against the wall. She and Kelly stood stock still, listening. 'Snoring?' Megan turned to Kelly for a sign that she wasn't mistaken.

Kelly nodded. From somewhere under the bundle of rags on the floor a faint rumble was coming. She leaned forward, glancing at the fingers of her right hand as if steeling herself to touch the evil-smelling bundle.

'Do you want me to?' Megan squeezed past her. It wasn't fair to make poor Kelly deal with this. She was the one who had insisted on coming here. And she had come across far worse sights and smells in the mortuary in Birmingham.

'Cora!' Megan bent down and shook what looked like the shape of a shoulder. She felt the warmth of flesh beneath the rough blanket. It moved under her hand but there was no sound, other than the gentle snoring.

'Cora, time to wake up!' She pulled the blanket away and saw that it was the woman's leg she had been shaking. She recognised the stained skirt from last night. Megan wondered if Cora had any other clothes. She glanced around the gloomy shed. There was no furniture. Apart from a couple of unopened lager cans and a half empty whisky bottle there was nothing at all apart from the woman and the tatty blanket she was wrapped in.

'Cora!' She was almost shouting now. There was a grunt and a couple of slurred words that Megan couldn't make out.

A pair of bloodshot eyes opened and Cora McBride raised herself on one elbow. 'Who the hell are you?' she snarled, the Scottish accent thickened by her hangover.

'I'm Pauline's friend.' Megan tried to help her sit up, but Cora shrugged her off. 'Remember last night?' she coaxed. 'Pauline was giving you a lift home.'

'Nah!' Cora shook her head violently. 'She bloody didna! Shanks' bloody pony got me back last night!'

Megan glanced at Kelly, who shrugged her shoulders.

'Wassamarra?' Cora rose slightly and slumped her back against the wall of the shed. She eyed Kelly suspiciously. 'What's she doin' here?'

'Cora,' Megan said, 'we're trying to find Pauline. We're worried about her. What happened last night, after you got in her car? Can you remember?'

Cora scratched her head. 'She went off somewhere . . . I dunno . . .'

'Went off?'

'Yeah. Left me in the friggin' car, all on ma tod.'

Megan frowned. 'Why did she do that?'

'How the hell should *ah* know!' Cora threw up her hands, almost falling sideways onto the floor.

'Did she go with someone? Did someone come to the car?' Megan could see Kelly's face out of the corner of her eye. Her lips were moving but no sound was coming out, as if she was prompting Cora, willing her to say more.

'Her mobile.' Cora nodded, her whole upper body swaying back and forth with the movement. 'Tha's what it war! The mobile goes and out she goes.'

At that moment a shrill sound rang out, making Megan jump. It was her own mobile. Her hand fumbled in her pocket. 'Hello?'

'Dr Rhys?'

She recognised the voice but couldn't place it.

'Sergeant Mullen. Vice. We met last night, remember? I'd like to ask you a few questions . . .'

'About Pauline Barrow?' Megan could feel her throat go tight as she said her name.

'I think it's highly likely that you were the last person to see her alive.' His tone was smug, with no trace of sympathy.

'No, I wasn't actually.' She almost spat out the words. 'In fact, I've just been speaking to the last person who saw her. It seems Pauline got a call on her mobile just before she disappeared.' There was a pause while she let this news sink in. 'I presume you're checking that out?'

There was silence at the other end.

'Not possible, I'm afraid,' Mullen said at last. 'There was no mobile in the handbag we found beside the body. Whoever killed her must have taken it.'

CHAPTER SEVEN

Megan stood in the doorway of the shed, one foot on the muddy ground. 'We shouldn't leave her like this,' she whispered to Kelly.

'She won't go anywhere else.' Kelly shrugged. 'Pauline tried loads of times—got her a place in a hostel, but she wouldn't take it.'

'Piss off now, the pair of ye!' Cora's voice boomed from the darkness. They heard her body shuffling onto the floor, heard a muffled curse as she pulled the blanket back over her head. A few seconds later she was snoring again.

'Come on.' Megan glanced at Kelly. 'I'll take you back.'

Leaving Cora McBride felt like a betrayal. Megan made a silent promise to come back. She would try to do what Pauline would have wanted. But first she had to find Pauline's killer.

As they picked their way back up the path she thought about Sergeant Mullen. He'd said he still wanted to talk to her, but he could wait a bit longer for his interview. She needed to ask Kelly some questions. Find out what had gone on last night between her sister and that pimp. 'Tell you what,' she said as Kelly climbed into the car, 'when you've picked your daughter up from school I'll run you both home.'

Kelly looked at her. 'It's okay—you don't have to do that.'

'Oh, it's no trouble.' Megan wasn't going to take no for an answer. 'It's the least I can do after taking you so far out of your way.'

'Okay. Thanks.' Kelly flashed her a tight smile. It was clear she wasn't sure of her. Perhaps she guessed that Megan's real reason for giving her a lift home was to check up on her sister. But if she did suspect, she didn't say anything. She kept quiet for the whole journey to the school, only opening her mouth to say 'right' or 'left'.

When they reached the gates Kelly jumped out. A pretty little girl of about six or seven ran up to her. She had pale brown skin and wore a pink summer dress, her black hair caught up in silver slides.

Kelly climbed into the back of the car with her. 'This lady's giving us a lift home,' was all she said by way of an introduction.

The child sat as quiet as a mouse as her mother directed Megan to a council estate a few streets from the school. The houses were all painted a yellow-brown colour that made Megan think of the nicotine stains on

Pauline Barrow's fingers. The plaster on the walls was crumbling in places and the gardens were full of litter. They pulled in by a house with an old double bed lying upside down on the patch of lawn, its springs sticking out at crazy angles.

'It's not that one,' Kelly said, her mane of blonde hair flying out as she jerked her head. 'It's the next one along.'

Megan inched the car further along the kerb. The garden of number sixty-eight looked tidier than the ones on either side, but the front door had a panel missing. Someone had taped a piece of cardboard over the hole.

'BJ did that last night, didn't he, Mam?' the little girl piped up.

Megan could see her face in the rear view mirror. Her small nose was wrinkled in a frown.

'He's a naughty boy, isn't he?' She jumped out of the car before her mother could answer, ran up the path and rang the doorbell.

Kelly was still in the car. Megan could see her in the mirror now, her lips parting and closing as if she couldn't make up her mind what to say.

From the corner of her eye Megan saw the front door open. She turned her head and caught sight of Tracy Jebb. The woman was only there for a split second but it was long enough for Megan to see the damage that had been done to her.

Tracy's face was a mass of purple bruises. Her eyes were so swollen they were nothing more than slits.

'My God!' Megan turned in her seat so she was facing Kelly. 'What happened here last night?'

Kelly didn't answer. She was staring at the seat in front of her.

'Kelly, please,' Megan coaxed. 'I know BJ found the card Pauline gave to Tracy . . .' She let the words hang in the air. Kelly must know that BJ was a prime suspect for Pauline's murder. Why would she cover for him? Why would she want to let him get away with doing that to her sister?

'He's threatened you, hasn't he?' Megan's voice was almost a whisper. She held her breath, watching Kelly's face. The girl nodded, a quick movement that was more like a twitch, as if she was afraid of someone in the street seeing her.

'What did he say?'

Kelly's eyes darted left and right before she opened her mouth. 'He said he'd take Shanice.'

'Shanice?'

'That's his daughter by Tracy.' Kelly bit her lip. 'I came downstairs when he was hitting her. I was . . . so scared. I just stood there, hiding behind the door. I wanted to scream at him to stop doing that to Tracy but I knew that if I did he'd start on me.' A deep flush spread up her neck to her face. 'He saw me when he was leaving. He grabbed me by the hair and shoved me up against the wall.' Her voice was shaking and Megan could see tears welling in her eyes. 'That's when he said it.'

'Kelly, we have to go to the police.'

'No!' Kelly grabbed her bag and reached for the handle of the door. 'I've already said too much!'

'But they'll help you.' Megan caught her arm, her eyes pleading. 'If you let him get away with it he'll carry on doing it.'

Kelly was pulling away, the door half-open now.

'What if he's the one who murdered Pauline?' Megan hissed. 'How long before he does the same to Tracy? Or to you, Kelly?'

Kelly paused, one leg out of the car. Again she glanced this way and that, like a nervous bird watching for a cat. 'The police?' she hissed back. 'You really think they give a stuff?' She tossed her head as she turned to look Megan in the eye. 'Oh, they say all those things, like they're going to put you in a safe house, give you protection and all that . . .' She tailed off, her mouth turning down at the edges in a look of disgust.

'Kelly, I'll bloody well *make* them if I have to!'

The women looked at each other. Megan's eyes were blazing. Kelly's were narrow with anger and glassy with unshed tears.

'Please do this,' Megan whispered. 'Think of your daughter. Do you really want her growing up in a house where this sort of thing goes on night after night?'

For a second Kelly hesitated. Then, in one swift movement, she jumped out of the car. 'I'm sorry,' she called over her shoulder. 'I can't do it. I just *can't.*'

She slammed the door behind her. Megan watched her disappear through the broken front door. She sat for a moment, wondering whether to follow. Perhaps she could persuade Tracy to go to the police instead. Instinct told her it would be a waste of time. Of the two sisters Kelly was the brave one, and if she was afraid of dishing the dirt on BJ . . .

Megan turned the key in the ignition. There was nothing for it. She was going to have to go to Sergeant Mullen and tell him everything she knew. Tell him about BJ throwing the card at Pauline and about the beating he'd given Tracy.

Even if he wasn't Pauline's killer they ought to arrest him for GBH on Tracy. What was it Pauline had said about Mullen? *Doesn't give a toss what the pimps'll do to them if they find out who's dropped them in it.* Well, this was going to be his wake-up call. If he wouldn't lock BJ up, she'd go over his head. *Make* someone listen.

She pulled an A-Z of Cardiff out of the glove compartment and flicked over the pages, working out the best route to the police station. It was coming up to rush hour and she didn't want to get stuck in traffic.

A couple of minutes later she was on her way, driving slowly and concentrating on the names of the streets. Some were hard to read. They were covered in graffiti and one had had a pot of blue paint thrown all over it.

Despite the grim look of the houses there were some very flash cars parked in the roads outside. She passed a red Mercedes Convertible in one street, and as she turned a corner a shiny black American import pulled out behind her.

It wasn't until she reached the turning for the main road that she got the feeling she was being followed. Pulling up at the traffic lights she glanced in the mirror. There was something familiar about the car—that big spoiler on the front. Suddenly she remembered. It was the Dodge Crossfire—the one that had pulled up outside the café last night. She glanced at the man behind the wheel. Even though he was wearing shades he seemed to be staring straight at her.

She was sure this was BJ. Had he been watching her when she pulled up at Kelly's house? Had he been waiting to see if she would go inside? She felt a stab of fear in her stomach. Had she made things worse by taking Kelly and her daughter home? She swallowed hard. At least if he's following me, she thought, he can't be doing anything to them.

Despite the heavy traffic he stuck to her like glue. Every time she pulled up at a junction or a red light he was there. His lips were parted in a smug smile that showed his teeth. When the sun came out from behind a cloud a flash of light seemed to shoot from his mouth, as if he was firing some sort of laser beam at her. She blinked and pulled away as the traffic lights changed. Then it dawned on her. He must have a diamond in one of his front teeth.

She thought about the way Jackie Preston had described the man who knifed her. She'd told the police he wore shades and had a local accent. Surely she would have noticed if he'd had a diamond in his teeth? And that car—it was so distinctive with those spoilers and the alloy wheels—surely it would have stuck in Jackie's mind?

They were nearly at the police station now. She wondered what to do. If she pulled up in the street he might try to get at her when she opened the car door. Was that likely, though? In broad daylight, outside a police station?

She got the feeling he was just trying to scare her, the way he'd scared Kelly. He wanted her to know that he could follow her anywhere now because he knew her car. Whatever she said inside the police station, he would be waiting for her when she came out. So she'd better make damn sure she got Mullen on his case before she went anywhere else.

When she parked the car he pulled in behind her. Her hand was trembling as she reached for the handle of the door. Her ears strained, listening for his door to open. She heard nothing but the hum of traffic in the main road up ahead. But as she walked towards the police station she couldn't help herself. She had to look behind her, check that he wasn't there.

As she turned her head she caught the flash of a diamond behind the windscreen of his car. This time it wasn't coming from his teeth. It was coming from a large ring on his right hand, which he was lifting from the wheel to give her a little wave.

I'll get you, you bastard, she muttered. *I'll wipe that bloody smile off your face.*

CHAPTER EIGHT

Megan sat on a hard plastic chair in the foyer of the police station. There was a young lad of about fourteen, with a black eye, two seats along from her. He'd been sitting with a teenage girl and a baby in a pushchair, but the girl had gone outside for a cigarette, taking the baby with her.

Megan stared at a poster on the wall in front of her, waiting for Sergeant Mullen to call her through. But she kept glancing at the door. She'd half-expected BJ to follow her in. She could just imagine him sitting in the chair opposite, giving her the evil eye, trying to scare her out of talking to Mullen.

With a sudden, loud creak the heavy wooden door by the desk swung open. Megan saw something long and metal coming through it, then a woman's head, bent over so that her hair covered her face. The woman was on crutches, her right leg in plaster. As she limped towards the glass front door, Megan went to hold it open. The woman turned to thank her and Megan saw with a shock that it was a face she recognised.

It was Cheryl Parry, the woman she and Pauline had seen climbing into a car in the red light district last night. Pauline had said she thought her pimp had done that to her. And she'd said the woman's pimp was BJ.

Megan stared after Cheryl Parry as she hobbled off down the street. Had she come here to dish the dirt on BJ? And if so, what would he do if he caught sight of her coming out of the police station?

Suddenly it struck her that BJ might not have been following her at all. He might have been on his way to the station because he'd got wind of Cheryl coming here to shop him. It could have been pure chance that he set off at the same time she was leaving Tracy and Kelly's house.

The door had swung shut but she pushed it open, stepping out into the street. She felt a strong urge to run after the woman, to warn her that BJ was parked just round the corner. But as she did so she heard her name called in the foyer.

She stood rooted to the spot, her eyes darting to the foyer and then back to Cheryl Parry. Then, to her relief, she saw the woman cross the road. She was making for the taxi rank, away from where BJ was waiting. He wouldn't see her. She was safe.

Five minutes later Megan was shown into an interview room where Sergeant Mullen was sitting with a young police woman. On a table in the corner she could see something red and shiny with a big silver buckle in a see-through plastic evidence bag. The sight of it made her go cold. It was Pauline Barrow's handbag.

'You saw Cheryl Parry on her way out?' Mullen raised one eyebrow as he spoke, not waiting for her to answer. 'Right waste of bloody time that was!' His eyebrow dropped and two deep lines appeared above his nose. 'And it'll be the same old story with Tracy Jebb. I've tried twice in the past six months to get BJ for GBH on Tracy.' He rolled his eyes at the strip light on the ceiling. 'I've seen it time and time again with these girls—we get to court and at the last minute they go and drop the charges.'

Megan could feel the heat in her chest and neck as anger surged inside her. Pauline had been right. Mullen didn't give a toss about those women. He'd written them off before she'd had a chance to say a word about what BJ had done.

'Don't you think that's because they were frightened?' she said. 'BJ's a very violent man—don't you offer them protection when they come to you?'

'We give them panic buttons in their houses, but they don't use them.' He shrugged. 'They're just mugs, these girls. We can't touch BJ unless we get some hard forensic evidence.' His eyes flicked across to the red handbag lying in the corner. 'But I'm *hoping* he's just dropped himself right in it.'

Megan's eyes narrowed. 'What do you mean?'

Mullen and the police woman exchanged glances. 'When they found Pauline's body there was something in her mouth . . .' He tailed off, his nostrils twitching like a dog scenting a rabbit.

'What?'

Megan felt her own mouth go dry as Mullen told her about the condoms.

'We've just had word from the lab,' he said. 'One of them has semen inside it. We'll have to wait for a DNA result, obviously . . .'

His words hung in the air. There was no need for him to finish the sentence. It was plain that he'd got BJ down as the killer. As she sat staring at his smug face Pauline's words came drifting back into her mind: *It'd be very handy for the cops if they could pin it on him. Mullen's had him in his sights for weeks.* Pauline had been talking about the Jackie Preston case, but she could just as easily have been talking about her own murder. Mullen looked set to finger BJ for the lot.

'So in the meantime you do nothing?' She held his gaze. 'On the basis of a DNA match you *might* get, you call off the search?'

Mullen's face darkened. 'I didn't say that.'

'But you meant it.' She folded her arms and leaned back in her chair. 'God knows I'm all for getting BJ behind bars—the sooner the better—but shouldn't you be casting the net a bit wider before you jump to conclusions?' She saw his jaw tense. She knew that she'd hit a raw nerve but she wasn't going to leave it alone. 'There must be other pimps who hated Pauline just as much as BJ,' she went on. 'I mean, the other night, some guy came cruising past us in a car with blacked out windows and hurled abuse at her. There could be any number of men like that.'

She heard him take a deep breath. 'And it's a safe bet we'll have all their DNA on record—so if it's not BJ, we'll know soon enough.'

'But in the meantime some maniac could be out there about to kill again!' Megan was trying not to raise her voice. 'There's loads more you should be doing. What about Pauline's mobile phone? Have you tried putting a trace on it?'

'Done that.' His voice was tight and his eyes were fixed on the ceiling. 'No signal—I should think it's been chucked in the Bay.'

Megan's chair scraped loudly as

she pushed it back and stood up. 'I'd like to see Inspector Cameron,' she said, her eyes flashing as they met his.

'Oh?' He pressed his lips between his teeth, making the skin go white. 'Can I ask why?'

God, isn't it obvious? The muscles of her face clenched tight as she stopped herself saying the words out loud. She took a breath before she spoke: 'BJ followed me here. He saw me outside Tracy Jebb's house. He's knows I've been talking to you . . .' She trailed off. *And you're doing sod all about it*, was what she wanted to say.

Instead she turned to the young police woman. 'Would *you* want to go home with a maniac like that on your tail?' The WPC looked away. She glanced at Mullen, who shrugged.

'I've told you,' he said, shifting in his seat. 'We've got nothing on him. Not yet. It's a waiting game.'

'Well I'm sorry, but *I'm* not

prepared to wait.' Megan sat down again, staring him out. 'I want something done—and if you won't do it I'll go over your head.'

Mullen turned to the police woman. 'Look after Dr Rhys for me, will you?' he said. Without a word to Megan he left the room.

There was an awkward silence. The WPC had her eyes fixed on the table between them. At last she said: 'Can I get you a coffee?'

As the door closed behind her Megan's eyes fell on the plastic evidence bag in the corner of the room. *Pauline's handbag*, she thought. *They've left me alone in the room with Pauline's handbag...*

It was too much to resist. In three quick strides she was across the room. She dug in her pocket for a tissue, wrapping it over her hand to avoid leaving fingerprints. Fumbling with the evidence bag, she glanced over her shoulder. The WPC would be back any minute. She had to be quick.

Snapping open the catch she peered into the pale, silky inside of the handbag. There it was. The thing she was looking for: a bunch of keys. There was a car key and two others. One of them had to be the key to Pauline's flat.

She fished the keys out and stuffed them into her pocket. In another couple of seconds the handbag was back in its plastic case and she was back in her seat.

Her heart thumped as she waited for the police woman to return. What she had done was theft. She could get arrested if they found out. But if Mullen wasn't going to do it, somebody had to. Going to Pauline's home should have been top of his list. There could be all kinds of clues there: clues to who might have wanted her dead.

When the door opened it was Cameron's face that she saw. He gave her a polite nod and stood aside to let the WPC through with a tray of coffee.

Megan fingered the keys in her pocket as she went through the whole story again for Cameron. She needed to get to Pauline's place without having to worry about being followed by BJ. To do that she had to persuade the Inspector to pull BJ in.

But Cameron was having none of it. He was a lot nicer about it than Mullen—all charm and very, very polite—but when it came to the crunch he was saying exactly the same as his sergeant: he didn't want to risk screwing things up by arresting BJ without hard forensic evidence.

The best he could offer was protection for Megan and the Jebb sisters. He promised to put a watch on Tracy and Kelly's house and he offered to drive Megan home himself.

'You can leave your car here,' he said. 'I'll get someone to follow us in an unmarked car and you can borrow that for the next couple of days—at least until the DNA results come through.'

She thought for a moment before she replied. It wasn't what she had wanted but it was better than nothing. 'Okay,' she said. 'Can we go now?' The sooner she could get to Pauline's the better.

Cameron's car smelt of his aftershave. It was a pleasant smell. Hugo Boss, she guessed, or maybe Calvin Klein. As he did up his seat belt she saw his eyes close up for the first time. They were deep blue and he had great lashes for a man—dark and thick.

Was it guilt about taking the keys that made her feel so uneasy when he looked at her? Or was it something else? Something she didn't want to admit to? He was very good-looking—she couldn't deny that. But she was damned if she was going to let him charm his way out of this.

'Your sergeant told me about the condoms in Pauline's mouth.' She turned her head towards him and he nodded. 'How exactly did she die?'

After he had explained she said: 'Do you really think Pauline Barrow and Jackie Preston were attacked by the same person?'

He glanced in the rear view mirror before replying: 'Clearly you don't?'

'I think it's unlikely.' She counted off the evidence on her fingers. 'Okay, one or two things seem the same—they were both stabbed and both attacks took place in the red light district. But Jackie was stabbed more than a dozen times in the face and neck. You said Pauline was stabbed just once in the stomach.'

Cameron nodded but said nothing.

'Jackie was attacked by a man who pulled up in a car,' she went on, 'but Pauline got a call from someone on her mobile.'

'And whoever stabbed her didn't

do it in a car,' Cameron agreed. 'The pathologist said it happened in the alley where she was found.'

'And another thing,' Megan said. 'Jackie's attacker drove off without even waiting to find out if she was dead. But Pauline's killer stayed around long enough to arrange her body and stuff those condoms in her mouth.'

'That was weird, I admit,' he said. 'I've never come across anything like that before. I got a call from the pathologist just before I came to see you. He'd been checking Pauline's gullet to see if she'd choked on the condoms. But no—he says they were definitely put in her mouth after she was killed.'

'It's as if her death was some kind of sick joke.' Megan glanced at him as he swung the car round a bend. 'It must have been planned very carefully. But Jackie's attack seems like more of a spur-of-the-moment thing—like someone losing it and just lashing out.'

'I know.' Cameron was shaking his head slowly. 'And that description Jackie gave bothers me.' He shot her a quick look. 'Certainly didn't sound like BJ.'

Megan took a few seconds to reply. She was trying to weigh him up. She'd thought he was right behind Sergeant Mullen, but now she wasn't so sure. 'What worries me,' she said slowly, 'is that Sergeant Mullen seems to think it's an open-and-shut case. So much so that he's called off the search.'

Cameron pulled up at a red light. He stared straight ahead, saying nothing.

Why won't he answer, she wondered? *Is he just being loyal to a fellow copper, or does he know something he's not letting on?*

CHAPTER NINE

It was dark by the time Cameron got Megan home. After he'd pulled up outside he turned to her, his lips parting, as if there was something very urgent he wanted to say.

The way he was looking at her made her feel strange. It was the kind of look Jonathan had given her the night everything changed: the night they'd ended up in bed together at his hotel.

She blinked away the memory. A flash of headlights told her that the officer who had followed them had just pulled up behind.

'I'll get the keys off Chris,' Cameron said, 'and then I'll see you up to your door.'

'No, it's okay,' she said, 'you don't have to do that—I'll be fine.'

That look again. As if he wanted something more. Was it some sort of game? Was he turning on the charm to get her on his side? And whose side was he on, anyway?

'Are you sure?'

She gave a quick nod, avoiding his eyes. Then he was out of the car. By the time she'd gathered up her bag and got out he was back, holding the door open for her, the keys to the other car dangling from his fingers.

'We'll give it a couple of minutes,' he said, jerking his head up at the flat. 'Any problems, call me, okay?'

With a curt word of thanks she took the keys and left him standing on the pavement.

As soon as she opened the door of Jonathan's flat she knew something was wrong. The light was on in the lounge. She knew she hadn't left it on. Her eyes darted across to the sofa. A beige trench coat was slung across one of the arms. And there was a briefcase propped against the coffee table. Her heart thudded. Were those Jonathan's things? There were flashy silver buckles on the sleeves of the coat. She couldn't imagine him in something like that.

A sudden rush of sound made her jump. It was coming from the bathroom. Someone had turned on the shower. She stood rooted to the spot. Should she ring Cameron? How stupid she would look if it turned out to be Jonathan in there.

As her eyes flicked nervously around the room, she caught sight of a yellow cardboard folder on the coffee table. She stepped closer. There was a name in bold type across the top. Janie Northcliffe. Her stomach flipped over. It was the woman who had left the message on the answer phone: Jonathan's old girlfriend.

The heat of rage spread up her body to her face. She must have a key, then. After all this time she *still* had a key. And she'd had the cheek to let herself in and take a shower!

If Jonathan had walked into the

room at that moment she would have hit him. She took a step towards the bathroom, ready for a slanging match. But then she stopped. What if Jonathan didn't know about this? Janie couldn't have called him on his mobile because there was no signal at the place he was staying in Jamaica. What if he'd forgotten he ever gave her a key to his flat?

Then another voice started up inside her head. It was a voice that sounded like her mother: 'You haven't got time for this,' it said. 'There are more important things to do.'

The muscles in Megan's jaw tightened as she turned round and headed for the hall. Pulling open a cupboard she spotted what she was looking for: the big red mains electric switch. With a flick of her wrist she turned it off.

As she closed the door of the flat she caught the tail end of a scream. Janie Northcliffe had been plunged into total darkness in a shower that had turned stone cold. Megan couldn't resist a little smile of triumph.

When she reached the street she looked for Cameron's car, but it had gone. She ran across to the place where the other car had been left for her. Turning on the engine she glanced at the clock on the dashboard. Nine-fifteen. In the red light district the women would be out on the streets. She had to get to Pauline's killer before he got to anyone else.

It took her half an hour to drive to the area where Pauline had lived. Megan had never been given the exact address—all she knew was that Pauline had lived in a flat in a place called The Broadlands. She hadn't realised that The Broadlands was three high-rise blocks that housed hundreds of people.

She tried asking a couple of kids who were kicking a can around outside the lift. They said they had no idea who Pauline Barrow was, or which flat had been hers.

As Megan stared at the rows of balconies above her she realised she was wasting her time. The police would know the address, of course, but if she asked them they'd know she'd taken the keys from Pauline's bag.

She tried calling the number of the charity Pauline had worked for but all she got was an answer-phone message. Of course, she thought, it's after hours—there's no one there.

There was only one other way to find out. She got back in the car, heading for the red light district. One of the girls would know. Someone Pauline had tried to help. All she had to do was find a face she recognised.

As she drove towards the industrial estate she got the feeling, once again, that she was being followed. When she stopped at traffic lights she peered into the rear view mirror but it was impossible to make out anything in the glare of the headlights.

She felt a prickle of fear. What if BJ was on her tail again? Could he have spotted her leaving the police station in Cameron's car? She slowed as she passed the entrance of the industrial estate and the car behind her turned off. She breathed a sigh of relief.

Cruising slowly along, she scanned the doorways of the factories, looking for the shapes of women in the shadows. It was hard to make out their faces. But suddenly she saw a figure she knew. Cheryl Parry was leaning against a lamp post, her broken leg stuck out in front of her and her crutches slung over one arm.

'You don't know me,' Megan said as the woman leaned in at her open window, 'but I'm a friend of Pauline's—can you help me?'

'I never knew where she lived,' Cheryl said, after Megan had explained, 'but I know someone who did.' She jerked her head towards the corner of the street. 'Turn left up there. Outside the timber yard—that's where she stands.'

'What's her name?'

'Rosa,' Cheryl replied. 'She's Pauline's daughter—didn't you know?'

Of course! Megan cursed under her breath as she drove away. Why hadn't she thought of it herself?

She decided to park the car and approach Rosa on foot. Knowing how bad things had been between mother and daughter, she was going to have to handle this with great care.

Rosa was exactly where Cheryl had said she'd be, standing under the lit-up sign at the entrance to the timber yard, a cigarette in her hand. There was something about the way she stood that made Megan do a double take. From a distance she looked so much like Pauline it was like seeing a ghost.

'Excuse me . . .'

The face that turned towards Megan was scary. Rosa had big eyes with dark circles under them. Her skin was so pale it seemed to glow white in the light of the sign above her head. Her eyes couldn't seem to focus. She looked like someone who had been in a deep sleep and didn't want to wake up.

'You're Rosa, aren't you?' Megan went on.

The woman sniffed. 'Who's asking?'

'Megan. Megan Rhys. I was a friend of Pauline's.' She held out her hand but Rosa ignored it. 'She told me about you. Do you . . .' Megan hesitated. 'You know she's dead?'

The words hung in the air. Rosa's eyes dropped. She shuffled her feet. Then she looked straight at Megan, her eyes hard and full of anger. 'I had heard, yeah.'

'I worked with your mum.'

Megan's voice was soft and low, as if she was calming a child about to throw a tantrum. 'I want to try and find the person who killed her. Will you help me?'

Rosa frowned. She said nothing.

'I need to know where she lived.' Megan mentally crossed her fingers. 'I've got the keys to her flat, but I don't know which one it is.'

Something flickered in the woman's eyes. 'I *could* take you, I s'pose,' she said, glancing up and down the empty street, 'but you'd have to make it worth my while.'

She didn't have to spell it out. She wanted money, of course, for the punters she'd be missing out on if she went to the flat. Not that there were many about tonight, from what Megan had seen.

'Okay.' Megan took two twenty pound notes from her purse. 'Will that cover it?'

With another loud sniff Rosa snatched the money from her hand.

'I s'pose,' she said. 'Where's your wheels?'

As they pulled away from the timber yard, a car nosed out of a side street. Megan didn't see it. It wasn't close enough for her to realise she was being followed. The driver seemed to know exactly where she was headed.

*   *   *

When they pulled up outside the flats Rosa jumped out of the car. Before Megan could follow she'd disappeared. Megan cursed herself for being so stupid. She should have made her give her the address before handing over the money. She paced up and down, wondering whether to go and search for Rosa. Roaming about this place in the dark was asking for trouble.

It was a shock when, a few minutes later, Rosa came out of the shadows. 'Come on,' she said, 'it's on the tenth floor.'

Megan followed her to the lift. Why was Rosa doing this? She'd obviously scored some drugs—why bother coming back? Did she have some feelings for her mother after all?

Rosa could hardly keep still as they waited for the lift. When the doors opened a wave of cannabis smoke and stale urine hit them.

'Come on,' Rosa said again, giving Megan a little push. 'It's number two-six-five. I'll show you.'

The lift seemed to take forever to reach the tenth floor. Rosa kept pressing the buttons, stamping her feet as she did it. The lift shuddered and Megan felt a surge of panic at the thought of being trapped with a junkie who was getting more edgy by the minute.

At last the lift doors opened. Rosa led the way down a dingy landing. It looked as if someone had dragged a burst bin bag along the floor. As

Megan fumbled with the keys Rosa shuffled from one foot to the other.

'I'll come in and help you look, if you like.' Rosa went through the door ahead of her.

Why is she still here? The words drummed in Megan's head. Letting this woman into Pauline's flat felt all wrong: like giving the keys to a burglar. But this was Pauline's daughter—her only relative—so how could she turn her out?

Megan glanced about her, keeping one eye on Rosa. Everything was clean and tidy and the walls looked newly painted. The cushions were plumped up and there was a vase of wilting pink carnations on the coffee table.

'Nice, innit?' Rosa plonked herself down on the sofa, resting her feet on the coffee table and almost knocking the vase over. Her eyes had changed. The wildness had gone. Now there was something else. A mean look. Was she jealous of what her mother had got?

A second later she jumped up, bounding over to the sliding glass door that opened onto a little balcony beyond. 'Bloody hot in here, though, eh?' she laughed.

It was very stuffy in the flat. The sun must have been beating down on that glass door all day. No wonder the flowers were drooping.

Rosa pushed the door open to let the cool night air into the room. She stood there, clutching the handle, staring. Suddenly it hit Megan. That mean smile, that twitch of the eyebrows. Rosa was waiting. Waiting for the penny to drop.

'You know, don't you?' As she said the words Megan felt her mouth go dry. 'You know who killed your mother.'

CHAPTER TEN

Rosa said nothing, just stared. Megan swallowed hard. She was thinking about the car that had tailed her to the red light district. Was it BJ? Had Rosa set her up?

She thought she heard something in the hall outside. Footsteps? She spun round. As she did so she saw a flicker of movement from Rosa. A glint of metal caught the light.

Christ! She's got a knife. Megan froze, her eyes fixed on the blade. Rosa took a step forward.

'Rosa . . .' Megan's voice was hoarse with fear. She was racking her brain for something to say: something to stop the woman coming any closer. 'Please . . . he's not worth it!'

Rosa's eyebrows flicked up. She made a sound that was a cross between a laugh and a snort. 'You think I'm doing this for BJ? For that pile of shit? Ha!' She stabbed the air with the knife. 'Why d'you think I went to all the trouble of getting a rubber full of his cum to stuff in the old tart's gob?' Her nostrils flared as she tossed her head. 'To drop the bastard in it, that's why! Killed two bloody birds with one stone!'

'You?' Megan blinked.'

'Yes—me!' Rosa's eyes glittered as she brought the tip of the knife level with her mouth. A slow smile parted her lips, showing small, crooked teeth. 'So bloody easy, it was. She was that desperate to make things up.' Her head cocked to one side and she rolled her eyes at the ceiling. *'Just call me, Rosa—any time.'* The voice was a mocking take-off of Pauline's. 'So I did.' She gave another grunt. 'I just called her mobile and she came running— stupid cow!'

Megan flinched as the knife whipped the air.

119

'But BJ—that was dead clever, you know?' Rosa's lips slid into a smug smile. 'Know how I done that?' She stared at the wall over Megan's shoulder, as if she was playing back the scene in her head. 'Give him a blow job, that's how. Spat it into a Durex and Bob's your uncle—'bye 'bye BJ!'

The knife flashed as Rosa held it up to Megan's neck.

'Put it down, Rosa.' She was trying to stop her voice from shaking, trying not to let on how terrified she was. Outside, somewhere far below, she could hear the hum of traffic. *Keep her talking*, Megan thought. *Keep her talking while you work out what to do.*

'You've fooled them, Rosa—you really have.' She could feel the blade against her throat as she spoke. 'They're going to lift him for stabbing Jackie Preston too—did you know?'

Their faces were inches apart. Megan saw the pupils of Rosa's eyes contract.

'Stupid bastard told me all about that.' She tapped the point of the knife with her finger. 'Said Jackie'd never tell 'cos he'd threatened to kill her kids if she did.' She gave a loud sniff. 'That's when I saw my chance. I knew if I did it right then, right after Jackie was done, they'd all think it was him.'

Megan's throat was bone dry. She wanted to swallow but the knife was pressing against her windpipe. 'Rosa,' she said, her voice a hoarse whisper, 'I know you felt let down by Pauline. I understand that—really I do.'

'She was so two-faced.' Rosa hissed. 'Thought she was Mother bloody Teresa! Couldn't do it for her own kid, though, could she? Couldn't care less when it really *mattered*!' She stared at Megan, her eyes like slits. 'Why did you have to come poking your nose in?'

'Rosa.' Megan felt the edge of the

121

knife graze her skin as she spoke. 'Please listen to me—killing me isn't going to make things any better. If you tell the police what you've told me . . .'

'Don't give me that shit!' She pulled the knife back and lunged at Megan's chest. Megan shot sideways, dropped to the floor and launched herself at the woman's legs. Rosa let out a cry of surprise and staggered backwards, her arms flailing. Megan made a grab for her wrist. But Rosa was stronger than she looked. With a yell she jerked her arm back, pulling Megan with her. Together they tumbled through the doorway onto the balcony.

Megan saw a sea of orange lights in the darkness. They made her feel giddy. As she fell onto the metal railings she felt Rosa's nails clawing at the flesh of her arm. There was a loud bang. And then nothing.

*   *   *

Afterwards, she couldn't remember how it happened. Was it the crash of the door that did it? Was it the sight of Cameron and his men storming the flat that made Rosa jump from the balcony? Or was it her doing? Had she pushed Rosa over the railings as she blacked out?

'You don't remember telling us about Jackie Preston, do you?' Cameron had a puzzled smile on his face. They were in his office—a big, sunny room with a stunning view of Cardiff Bay. 'You started mumbling something when the medics got you on the stretcher. None of us could tell what you were saying at first.'

Megan shook her head slowly. 'I think I was probably trying to tell you to get to Rosa: get her to tell you what she'd told me about BJ. I didn't know that she was already dead.'

Cameron nodded, a lock of brown hair falling across one eye. 'Well, we got him in the end—just repeating what you'd said was enough to make Jackie Preston talk—but you nearly got yourself killed.'

'You could have come earlier . . .' She gave him a look that was a cross between a smile and a frown. 'How did you know, anyway?'

He answered her with an upward flick of his eyebrows and a lopsided grin.

'Was it you in that car?'

He nodded. 'The CCTV picked up on you nicking Pauline's keys—we're not as stupid as we look, you know.'

There was an awkward silence. Megan was staring down at the table. She wasn't going to say sorry, because she wasn't sorry. Would the truth about Pauline's murder and Jackie Preston's stabbing ever have come out if she hadn't taken the keys? She doubted it.

She got to her feet, avoiding his eyes, aware that he had stood up too. 'Well,' she said, 'if there's nothing else . . . unless, of course, you're thinking of doing me for theft?'

'I don't think that's necessary, no.'

There was something about the way he said it that made her look up. He was staring at her in the same way he'd stared in the car the night Rosa died. As if he wanted to ask her something but couldn't quite bring himself to do it.

She hesitated for a fraction of a second. Did he want her to stay? Was he about to ask her to go for a drink with him or something? And if he did, what would she say?

'Was there something else?' She'd meant to say it in a neutral way, but somehow it came out wrong, as if she was fed up of him taking up her time.

'I . . . er . . . I wondered if you'd like to go for a meal sometime?' He blinked, and she could see that his cheeks were going pink. 'By way of a thank-you.'

'Oh, I . . .' She tailed off, feeling the colour rise in her own face. Part of her thought yes, why not? He was good-looking, charming . . . but somewhere inside her head a voice was saying no. Was it Jonathan? Was he the reason she didn't want to start anything with anyone else? She thought of that woman in his flat. Did he deserve any loyalty after that? She didn't know. But she did know that she missed him.

'I'm sorry.' She bit her lip. 'I've got to go back to Birmingham. Some trouble with one of my students— I've got to go and sort it out.' It was a lie. Something in his face told her that he knew this, but in a second his mask was back in place.

'Don't worry—I understand.' He smiled as he showed her out.

*   *   *

It was another six months before Megan went back to Cardiff. Jonathan had got into the habit of coming to her place at weekends, but now he was away again—in Australia this time. So it wasn't for him she'd returned to the city. She'd come back to see Kelly Jebb.

It was strange, watching her unload the condoms from the boot of her car, just the way Pauline had done.

'I knew you'd be great for this job,' Megan said as they sat in the greasy spoon café later on. 'Do you like it?'

Kelly nodded, pushing her long blonde hair back from her face. 'Getting off the game was the best thing that ever happened to me.' She grinned. 'I couldn't have done it without you putting a good word in, though—or without BJ behind bars.'

'How's Tracy?'

'Oh, getting there, you know?' Kelly shrugged. 'Took her a long time to believe it—that he wasn't coming after her.'

Megan nodded. 'And Cora?'

'Finally got her into a hostel.' Kelly rolled her eyes at the ceiling. 'Right case, she is. "I'll move out of the shed," she says, "but only 'cos it's so friggin' cold!" She's threatening to go back when the weather warms up—let's hope we can get her off the booze before then . . .' Kelly tailed off, rubbing her chin

'Pauline would be so proud of you, you know.'

Kelly's eyes clouded. 'Do you think so? It's all that keeps me going sometimes.' She traced a scratch in the table with her finger. 'You get so much shit. From the pimps, the police—even the girls sometimes— and you wonder if it's all worth it.'

'Oh, it is,' Megan said. She was staring out of the window into the darkness beyond. Watching cars slow to a crawl as they pulled onto the industrial estate. 'Believe me, it is.'